PENNY FRANCIS

YOUR FIRST STEPS

A Simple Guide For The New Believer

Other Titles by the Author

From Pen to Paper

My Affliction Has A Sound

Shame Is Not Your Portion

For more information visit:

www.pastorpennyfrancis.com

A Special Message

I decided to write this special message in case a curious soul — an unbeliever picked up this book... If that's you, then keep reading — the next few pages have been written with you in mind. Yes — this special message is just for you!

If you are already a believer then you may be able to think of someone who needs this book. If you're a new believer who has just started a new walk with Christ you can keep reading too... What you read will serve to confirm and reassure you as you take **Your First Steps** on this amazing Christian Journey.

Ok, let's get back to the curious one!... Perhaps you just happened to pick up this book and briefly glance through the pages and you are now thinking about putting it down, then don't — please keep reading! This could be the most important book you ever read...

The information in the pages of this book could be just what you have been looking for all your life. It may just provide you with answers to some of the questions you find yourself asking. Well, you've read the first few paragraphs — Why not keep reading? Who knows what you may find out, that will start you on the life path that for all kinds of reasons you've been reluctant to embark on before now. Perhaps you feel that this kind of life isn't for you or that your life is absolutely fine and you don't need to make any changes or adjustments to the way you live or how you conduct your personal affairs. It could be that your previous experiences of Christianity have been disappointing or confusing.

I have found over the years when having conversations with individuals that there are many reasons why Christianity may not seem right for them especially where some of the choices they will make are in conflict with or contrary to what would normally be in line with God's Word, the Bible.

I have also found that often individuals spend too much time comparing themselves to others when this life walk is meant to be a very personal one. This is what the Bible says, '*...continue to work out your salvation [that is, cultivate it, bring it to full effect, actively pursue spiritual maturity] with awe-inspired fear and trembling [using serious caution and critical self-evaluation to avoid anything that might offend God or discredit the name of Christ]—Philippians 2:12 (New International Version).* When we focus on our salvation walk from a personal perspective, life with Christ makes more sense and is definitely more rewarding.

So I thought it would be a good idea to briefly share the Good News — The Gospel of Jesus Christ. I suppose that I am not wrong in thinking that you have heard and read all kinds of different things about Jesus — some good and some bad! Hopefully, what you read today will give you a better perspective.

People often say it is easy for a 'bad' person to accept that they need to be saved (become a Christian) because they have done bad things and at some point they come to the realisation that they need God to forgive them and help them to live better lives. And those people who consider themselves to be 'good' don't think they need Jesus to save them because they don't believe they have done anything wrong! The truth of the matter is that taking the step of surrendering your life to Jesus Christ has nothing to do with whether you are 'good' or 'bad'. God makes it clear in His Word (The Bible) that *'everyone has sinned and we all fall short of God's holy standard'—Romans 3:23).* The only way to come up to God's standard is through Jesus Christ. The next verse makes this clear. *'Yet God, with undeserved kindness, declares that we are righteous. He did this through Christ Jesus when he freed us from the penalty for our sins. For God presented Jesus as the sacrifice for sin. People are made right with God when they believe that Jesus sacrificed his life, shedding his blood'—Romans 3:24-25.* If we accept this spiritual truth, we also accept that we are all sinners and condemned to death. *'For the wages of sin is death but the gift of God is eternal life'* —*Romans 6:23.*

The Good News is that Jesus Christ became a willing sacrifice so that we would not have to endure eternal separation from God in Hell. God loved us so much that He gave His only Son, Jesus, to bear our sins and die in our place. We see this explained in *2 Corinthians 5:21 'For God took the sinless Christ and poured into him our sins. Then, in exchange, he poured God's goodness into us!'(The Living Bible).* God demonstrated His love toward us by sending Christ to die for us while we were sinners (Romans 5:8).

Accepting and believing this to be true is just part of it. We also need to repent. God commands all people everywhere to repent (Acts 17:30). There are several variations mentioned in the Bible — "repent," "repented" and "repentance." They are found in the Bible over 100 times. Repentance is one of the steps to salvation. Repentance is feeling sincere regret or remorse which leads to a change of heart and mind toward God about your sin. When you come to this place in your heart and mind you agree with God that you are a sinner, and you also agree and accept what Jesus did for us on the Cross.

If you have read this far, why not take the next step? If you would like to accept Jesus into your life today you can do so by simply saying the Sinner's Prayer. The Sinner's Prayer (also called the Consecration Prayer and Salvation Prayer) is a Christian term referring to any prayer of repentance, prayed by individuals who feel convicted of the presence of sin in their lives. As a result they desire to form or renew a personal relationship with God through Jesus Christ. The Bible says in *Romans 10:9-10*, *'If you declare with your mouth, "Jesus is Lord," and believe in your heart that God raised him from the dead, you will be saved. For it is with your heart that you believe and are justified, and it is with your mouth that you profess your faith and are saved'* *(New International Version).*

Say this simple prayer sincerely from your heart:
Lord Jesus, for too long I've kept you out of my life.

I know that I am a sinner and that I cannot save myself. No longer will I close the door when I hear you knocking. By faith I gratefully receive your gift of salvation. I am ready to trust you as my Lord and Saviour. Thank you, Lord Jesus, for coming to earth. I believe you are the Son of God who died on the cross for my sins and rose from the dead on the third day. Thank you for bearing my sins and giving me the gift of eternal life. I believe your words are true. Come into my heart, Lord Jesus, and be my Saviour. Amen.** [The Sinner's Prayer by Dr. Ray Pritchard][1]

Congratulations and welcome to God's family. You are now a new Christian and I suppose you are wondering what to do next... Here are some suggestions:

■ Tell someone about the decision you made today to follow Jesus.

■ Pray every day — Talk to God. You don't have to use big words or complicated sentences. Just be Yourself!

■ Find a church and start to attend regularly — get connected.

■ Make sure that you get yourself a Bible and read it every day — You can't survive without God's Word.

Keep reading this book to learn more!

1   https://www.crosswalk.com/faith/prayer/prayers/the-sinners-prayer-4-examples.html

Contents

Penny Francis

Your First Steps

A Simple Guide For The New Believer

Introduction

I'm really excited about the decision you have made to embark on a new life with Jesus. It's early days but I just want you to know that you have become a part of God's family. This is confirmed in the Bible in Romans 9:8 — *'For his Holy Spirit speaks to us deep in our hearts and tells us that we really are God's children' (The Living Bible)*. So, welcome to God's family!

You have taken **Your First Steps** in that, you have accepted Jesus Christ as your personal Friend and have acknowledged him as your Saviour and Lord.

It is important that you read and study the Bible — God's Word, daily and apply it practically to your life. The Apostle Paul said *'Remember what Christ taught, and let his words enrich your lives and make you wise; teach them to each other and sing them out in psalms and hymns and spiritual songs, singing to the Lord with thankful hearts. And whatever you do or say, let it be as a representative of the Lord Jesus, and come with him into the presence of God the Father to give him your thanks.'—Colossians 3:16-17 (The Living Bible)*

Daily application of God's Word to your life will help you to grow spiritually and become more mature in your Christian walk and at the same time you will be establishing an eternal relationship with God as your Father, through Jesus Christ.

I pray that you are filled with God's wisdom and understanding as you read and study His Word. I hope you find **'Your First Steps'** a helpful resource and enjoy reading and personally applying its principles — The best of the rest of your life is ahead of you!

2 Corinthians 5:17... When someone becomes a Christian, he becomes a brand new person inside. He is not the same anymore. A new life has begun! (The Living Bible)

God's Word: Your Guide

Now that you have accepted Jesus Christ as your Lord, God's Word becomes your guide, in that it directs you in your new Christian life. In the following pages you will find relevant topics which have been chosen to help get you started. They will help you navigate through the scriptures and explore the various aspects of your new life in Christ. Each section also includes a list of specific Bible verses for you to read.

As you look to your future as a Christian, following the teachings of Jesus, please keep these words in mind. Jesus shared these words with the crowds that followed Him—*'Don't hide your light! Let it shine for all; let your good deeds glow for all to see, so that they will praise your heavenly Father.' Matthew 5:15-16 (The Living Bible)*

The words in Psalm 119:105 demonstrate how important God's Word is to us — *'Your words are a flashlight to light the path ahead of me and keep me from stumbling.' (The Living Bible)*

As a new Christian you may be wondering which part of the Bible you should read first. I would suggest starting with the Gospels — Matthew, Mark, Luke and John. They are found at the beginning of the New Testament — the second of two main sections of the Bible. I have found that many new Christians start with the Gospels of John or Luke.

There are lots of Bible Reading tools available on the internet — Bible Reading Plans which help you to read the Bible regularly in an organised way and 'Thoughts for the Day' material that include Bible verses which are good to use to start your day. These are just a couple that I can think of.

Also, there are Bible Apps that you can download to your phone, android or tablet devices which can provide a more convenient way to read your Bible. I have also found that sometimes the King James Version (KJV) can be hard to understand so it helps to read the Bible using a modern translation like the New International Version (NIV), New Living Translation (NLT) or The Living Bible (TLB). There are so many to choose from. I am sure you will soon find your own favourites as you begin studying the Bible for yourself. Below are some suggested Bible verses and passages you can also read to help you discover more about Jesus. Remember to read at your own pace, taking time for it to really sink in so you can understand what you are reading.

Genesis 1:1; Psalm 119:11; Matthew 22:37; John 5:24 Matthew 28:18-20; John 3:16; John 14:6; Romans 8:28; John 1:12; Romans 8:15; 1 John 3:1; Ephesians 2:8-10; Galatians 2:20; 1 Corinthians 15:3-4; Galatians 5:16; Colossians 1:27. Philippians 4:6-7; 2 Corinthians 5:17; Colossians 1:13-14; Colossians 2:13; 1 John 5:11-13; John 10:27-29 Ephesians 2:4-5

Personal Notes & Thoughts

Doubt, Disappointment & Discouragement

Doubts, Disappointments & Discouragements — Let's call them the 3 D's! They are just three of the many 'tests' of your faith which you will encounter as you progress in your new life as a Christian. Perhaps a time will come when you will experience doubts as to whether you are 'saved' or not. Perhaps you may wonder whether God hears you when you pray or feel uncertain about some other areas of your life. Perhaps life hasn't turned out quite how you expected. It's normal to experience challenging emotions as a Christian. However, the important thing for you to do is make sure that you do not allow yourself to be completely overwhelmed during those difficult times. Remember, that you can rely on Jesus to help you and don't forget to keep reading your Bible.

Remember that the word of God declares that you are saved because you have taken that first step in saying yes to Jesus. Don't worry about the Doubts, Disappointments or Discouragements or the other emotions and challenges you may face. Just remember that you have surrendered your future life into the hands of the Lord and He will be with you giving you His reassurance, peace and strength in those difficult moments.

Read what the Bible says...

2 Corinthians 5:7... *For we walk by faith, not by sight.*

Romans 10:10-13... *For with the heart man believeth unto righteousness; and with the mouth confession is made unto salvation. For the scripture saith, Whosoever believeth on him shall not be ashamed. For there is no difference between the Jew and the Greek: for the same Lord over all is rich unto all that call upon him. For whosoever shall call upon the name of the Lord shall be saved.*

2 Timothy 1:7... *For God did not give us a spirit of timidity (of cowardice, of craven and cringing and fawning fear), but [He has given us a spirit] of power and of love and of calm and well-balanced mind and discipline and self-control. (Amplified Bible)*

Deuteronomy 31:6... *Be strong and brave. Don't be afraid of them and don't be frightened, because the Lord your God will go with you. He will not leave you or forget you." (New Century Version)*

1 John 5:11-13... *And this is the record, that God hath given to us eternal life, and this life is in his Son. He that hath the Son hath life; and he that hath not the Son of God hath not life. These things have I written unto you that believe on the name of the Son of God; that ye may know that ye have eternal life, and that ye may believe on the name of the Son of God.*

Isaiah 41:10... *Fear thou not; for I am with thee: be not dismayed; for I am thy God: I will strengthen thee; yea, I will help thee; yea, I will uphold thee with the right hand of my righteousness.*

Jeremiah 29:11... *For I know the plans I have for you," declares the LORD, "plans to prosper you and not to harm you, plans to give you hope and a future. (New International Version)*

John 5:24... *Verily, verily, I say unto you, He that heareth my word, and believeth on him that sent me, hath everlasting life, and shall not come into condemnation; but is passed from death unto life.*

Romans 8:28... *And we know that in all things God works for the good of those who love him, who have been called according to his purpose. (New International Version)*

Personal Notes & Thoughts

Your Father Which Is In Heaven

Now that you are a child of God, you have automatically become a member of His family and like any loving and caring Father He wishes you to enjoy all the privileges and benefits which you are entitled to as His heir. He wants you to know that He knows everything about you and that He loves you very much.

It is important for you to understand that our heavenly Father gives very clear guidelines and directions about how we live in His family. Just like any normal family there are do's and don'ts that make for a good family life. His expectations are no different. Our heavenly Father is just like any parent who loves their children and does their best to teach them how to grow and become valuable members of society. This means that every now and then they will have to correct any behavior that is unacceptable. Our Father does the same for us. He corrects us or disciplines us so that we can be effective members of His Kingdom. God loves us so much that He pays special attention to our personal development and character. Also, as any good Father who loves His children, God has promised to give you His best gifts.

Read what the Bible says...

John 1:12... *But as many as received him, to them gave He power to become the sons of God, even to them that believe on his name.*

Romans 8:14... *For as many as are led by the Spirit of God, they are the sons of God.*

Colossians 1 v 12... *Giving thanks unto the Father, which hath made us meet to be partakers of the inheritance of the saints in light.*

Galatians 3:29... *And if ye be Christ's, then are ye Abraham's seed, and heirs according to the promise.*

Romans 8:17... *And if children, then heirs; heirs of God, and joint-heirs with Christ; if so be that we suffer with him, that we may be also glorified together.*

Hebrews 12:6... *The Lord disciplines those he loves, and he punishes everyone he accepts as his child. (New Century Version)*

Galatians 4:6, 7... *And because ye are sons, God hath sent forth the Spirit of his Son into your hearts, crying, Abba, Father. Wherefore thou art no more a servant, but a son; and if a son, then an heir of God through Christ.*

Matthew 7:11 ... *And if you hardhearted, sinful men know how to give good gifts to your children, won't your Father in heaven even more certainly give good gifts to those who ask him for them? (The Living Bible)*

James 1:17... *Every good action and every perfect gift is from God. These good gifts come down from the Creator of the sun, moon, and stars, who does not change like their shifting shadows. (New Century Version)*

Personal Notes & Thoughts

A Real Friend

Most people will usually agree that real friends are hard to find. A wonderful thing about you taking this step is that you now have Jesus as your personal Saviour and friend. Make Him your constant companion. He can be trusted more than any other friend. Jesus is the best example of true friendship that you could ever find. Think about all the qualities that you would expect to see in a best friend — Jesus has all those qualities and many more! He is the epitome of loyalty and has genuine concern for your well-being. He will be there for you when everyone else has abandoned you. He will never change on you — He will be a constant in your life. He will always be there to listen when you need to talk and He can be trusted 100%. Confide in Him, confess to Him, ask Him for whatever you need and love Him with all your heart, soul, mind and strength because He loves you so much more.

You can be confident in the friendship that Jesus offers — He will never ever let you down and He will never betray you. He is the best company you could ever have. Indeed He is the best friend you could ever have!

Read what the Bible says...

1 Peter 5 vs 6, 7... *Humble yourselves therefore under the mighty hand of God, that he may exalt you in due time: Casting all your care upon him; for he careth for you.*

Psalm 55:22... *Cast thy burden upon the Lord, and he shall sustain thee: he shall never suffer the righteous to be moved*

John 15:15... *I no longer call you slaves, for a master doesn't confide in his slaves; now you are my friends, proved by the fact that I have told you everything the Father told me. (The Living Bible)*

James 2:23... *And the Scripture was fulfilled which says, "Abraham believed God, and it was accounted to him for righteousness." And he was called the friend of God. (New King James Version)*

Mark 12:30... *Love the Lord your God with all your heart, all your soul, all your mind, and all your strength.' (New Century Version)*

Isaiah 26:3... *You, Lord, give true peace to those who depend on you, because they trust you. (New Century Version)*

Proverbs 17:17... *A friend loves you all the time, and a brother helps in time of trouble. (New Century Version)*

1 John 4:14... *And we have seen and do testify that the Father sent the Son to be the Saviour of the world.*

Proverbs 18:24... *There are "friends" who pretend to be friends, but there is a friend who sticks closer than a brother. (The Living Bible)*

John 15:13... *The greatest love a person can show is to die for his friends. (New Century Version)*

Personal Notes & Thoughts

The Liar & The Thief

The devil is the enemy of all Christians and he is a liar and a thief. He continually tries to deceive you and steal God's wonderful blessings from you. Whenever he gets an opportunity he uses it — he is always looking for your weaknesses. He uses your carnal and fleshly desires against you. He targets the areas in your life that you struggle with to tempt you back into a place of sin. He manipulates and plots against God's people to put us on a road to destruction. He will persecute you and make your life extremely difficult for the simple reason that this is his sole purpose against the children of God.

However, it is important for you to remember that the Lord said He will be with you always and therefore you have no reason to fear the devil or allow yourself to become susceptible to his evil schemes. You have to be willing to resist him and not give in or give up in spite of the many ways he attacks and comes against you.

Read what the Bible says...

John 10:10, 11, 27-29... *The thief cometh not, but for to steal, and to kill, and to destroy: I am come that they might have life, and that they might have it more abundantly. I am the good shepherd: the good shepherd giveth his life for the sheep. My sheep hear my voice, and I know them, and they follow me: And I give unto them eternal life; and they shall never perish, neither shall any man pluck them out of my hand. My Father, which gave them me, is greater than all; and no man is able to pluck them out of my Father's hand.*

1 John 3:8... *He that committeth sin is of the devil; for the devil sinneth from the beginning. For this purpose the Son of God was manifested, that he might destroy the works of the devil.*

1 Peter 5:8-11... *Be careful—watch out for attacks from Satan, your great enemy. He prowls around like a hungry, roaring lion, looking for some victim to tear apart. Stand firm when he attacks. Trust the Lord; and remember that other Christians all around the world are going through these sufferings too. After you have suffered a little while,* *our God, who is full of kindness through Christ, will give you his eternal glory. He personally will come and pick you up, and set you firmly in place, and make you stronger than ever. To him be all power over all things, forever and ever. Amen. (The Living Bible)*

Luke 10:19... *Behold, I give unto you power to tread on serpents and scorpions, and over all the power of the enemy: and nothing shall by any means hurt you.*

James 4:7... *So give yourselves completely to God. Stand against the devil, and the devil will run from you. (New Century Version)*

Personal Notes & Thoughts

Baptism: An Outward Show Of Inward Grace

Baptism is a special ceremony that Jesus instructed believers to participate in. The new Christian is immersed in water and then raised up to signify a personal identification and a public demonstration of the inward work of grace that has taken place in his/her life. Jesus was baptised, although sinless, giving us an example to follow. Through baptism we identify with the death, burial and resurrection of Jesus Christ. When we go under the water, it is symbolic of Christ's death on the cross and His burial in the tomb. When we are raised up out of the water it is symbolic of His resurrection from death. Water baptism testifies to the fact that we have turned away from our old life of sin to a new life in Jesus Christ. Being baptised publicly shows others that we have made a personal commitment to our new Christian life.

Baptism is also an act of obedience — in line with Jesus's commandment to the disciples in Matthew 28:19-20. When we go through water baptism we are acting in obedience to God's Word indicating that we are true followers or disciples of Jesus Christ.

Read what the Bible says...

Romans 6:3, 4... *Know ye not, that so many of us as were baptized into Jesus Christ were baptized into his death? Therefore we are buried with him by baptism into death: that like as Christ was raised up from the dead by the glory of the Father, even so we also should walk in newness of life.*

Matthew 28:19-20... *Go ye therefore, and teach all nations, baptizing them in the name of the Father, and of the Son, and of the Holy Ghost: Teaching them to observe all things whatsoever I have commanded you: and, lo, I am with you alway, even unto the end of the world. Amen.*

Mark 16:16... *He that believeth and is baptized shall be saved; but he that believeth not shall be damned.*

Acts 2:38... *Then Peter said unto them, Repent, and be baptized every one of you in the name of Jesus Christ for the remission of sins, and ye shall receive the gift of the Holy Ghost.*

Acts 8:12... *But when they believed Philip preaching the things concerning the kingdom of God, and the name of Jesus Christ, they were baptized, both men and women.*

Acts 18: 8... *And Crispus, the chief ruler of the synagogue, believed on the Lord with all his house; and many of the Corinthians hearing believed, and were baptized.*

Colossians 2:12... *Buried with him in baptism, wherein also ye are risen with him through the faith of the operation of God, who hath raised him from the dead.*

Personal Notes & Thoughts

Holy Communion

Holy Communion is another special ceremony that Christians participate in regularly. When Jesus was at supper with the disciples He instructed them to use bread and wine to commemorate the sacrifice that he was going to make when He died on the cross for our sins. The bread symbolises the broken body of Jesus and the wine symbolises His blood that was poured out for us.

There is no specific rule about how many times we receive Holy Communion in any given period. The early church participated in breaking of bread daily. Some churches partake every week and some once a month. Jesus simply said as often as you do this you remember my death until I return. The important point is that you do ensure that you receive Holy Communion. The church you attend will let you know when Holy Communion services are scheduled.

Read what the Bible says...

Luke 22:19-20... *And he took bread, and gave thanks, and brake it, and gave unto them, saying, This is my body which is given for you: this do in remembrance of me. Likewise also the cup after supper, saying, This cup is the new testament in my blood, which is shed for you.*

1 Corinthians 11:23-30... *That the Lord Jesus the same night in which he was betrayed took bread: And when he had given thanks, he brake it, and said, Take, eat: this is my body, which is broken for you: this do in remembrance of me. After the same manner also he took the cup, when he had supped, saying, This cup is the new testament in my blood: this do ye, as oft as ye drink it, in remembrance of me. For as often as ye eat this bread, and drink this cup, ye do shew the Lord's death till he come. Wherefore whosoever shall eat this bread, and drink this cup of the Lord, unworthily, shall be guilty of the body and blood of the Lord. But let a man examine himself, and so let him eat of that bread, and drink of that cup. For he that eateth and drinketh unworthily, eateth and drinketh damnation to himself, not discerning the Lord's body. For this cause many are weak and sickly among you, and many sleep.*

Acts 2:42... *And they continued stedfastly in the apostles' doctrine and fellowship, and in breaking of bread, and in prayers.*

Personal Notes & Thoughts

Fill Up With God's Word

Now that you have started out in your new life with Christ, you need spiritual food — The Word of God, to sustain you. Remember, your physical body cannot function properly when you abstain from food for a long period of time, i.e. if you don't eat regular meals. It's the same with your spiritual life. Therefore, you should feed on God's Word — read your Bible every day which helps to increase your faith and confidence in God. As you read and study the Bible, God will speak to you through His Word guiding and directing you.

Reading your Bible is a very important part of your daily Christian walk. It is through reading God's Word that you will learn more about Him and His purpose for your life.

Daily application of its spiritual truths will help you remain strong in your faith and conviction, giving you that assurance of God's presence in your life.

Attending Bible Study at your local church will help you to become more familiar with the Bible and also provides you with opportunities to share your thoughts and questions with fellow believers.

Read what the Bible says...

Matthew 4:4... *But he answered and said, It is written, Man shall not live by bread alone, but by every word that proceedeth out of the mouth of God.*

1 Peter 2:2... *Like newborn babies, long for the pure milk of the word, so that by it you may grow in respect to salvation (New American Standard Update)*

Psalm 119:9... *Wherewithal shall a young man cleanse his way? by taking heed thereto according to thy word.*

John 8:31, 32... *Then said Jesus to those Jews which believed on him, If ye continue in my word, then are ye my disciples indeed; And ye shall know the truth, and the truth shall make you free.*

Psalm 119:11... *I have thought much about your words and stored them in my heart so that they would hold me back from sin. (The Living Bible)*

James 1:21, 22... *Wherefore lay apart all filthiness and superfluity of naughtiness, and receive with meekness the engrafted word, which is able to save your souls. But be ye doers of the word, and not hearers only, deceiving your own selves.*

2 Timothy 3:16-17... *The whole Bible was given to us by inspiration from God and is useful to teach us what is true and to make us realize what is wrong in our lives; it straightens us out and helps us do what is right. It is God's way of making us well prepared at every point, fully equipped to do good to everyone. (The Living Bible)*

Joshua 1:8... *This book of the law shall not depart out of thy mouth; but thou shalt meditate therein day and night, that thou mayest observe to do according to all that is written therein: for then thou shalt make thy way prosperous, and then thou shalt have good success.*

Hebrews 4:12... *For whatever God says to us is full of living power: it is sharper than the sharpest dagger, cutting swift and deep into our innermost thoughts and desires with all their parts, exposing us for what we really are. (The Living Bible)*

2 Timothy 3:16-17... *All Scripture is given by God and is useful for teaching, for showing people what is wrong in their lives, for correcting faults, and for teaching how to live right. Using the Scriptures, the person who serves God will be capable, having all that is needed to do every good work. (New Century Version)*

Personal Notes & Thoughts

Prayer—Let's Have A Chat!

One of the most important responsibilities of your new life in Christ is Prayer. This is the way in which you establish a direct communication with God your Father — Praying in the name of Jesus. Constant prayer to your Father in heaven develops a successful and intimate relationship between you and Him.

Prayer is simply talking to God and listening for His voice. There are no right or wrong words — It's personal! Be thankful. Remember to pray for others. Ask the Lord to fill you with His Holy Spirit. Seek God's direction for your life daily.

You can pray to God at any time — with your eyes open or closed, kneeling, sitting or standing. God is always willing to listen. Your Christian life will not be fruitful and progressive without daily prayer.

Read what the Bible says...

1 Thessalonians 5:17... *Pray without ceasing.*

1 John 5:14, 15... *And this is the confidence that we have in him, that, if we ask any thing according to his will, he heareth us: And if we know that he hears us, whatsoever we ask, we know that we have the petitions that we desired of him.*

John 15:7, 8, 16... *If ye abide in me, and my words abide in you, ye shall ask what ye will, and it shall be done unto you. Herein is my Father glorified, that ye bear much fruit; so shall ye be my disciples. Ye have not chosen me, but I have chosen you, and ordained you, that ye should go and bring forth fruit, and that your fruit should remain: that whatsoever ye shall ask of the Father in my name, he may give it you.*

John 16:23, 24... *And in that day ye shall ask me nothing. Verily, verily, I say unto you, Whatsoever ye shall ask the Father in my name, he will give it you. Hitherto have ye asked nothing in my name: ask, and ye shall receive, that your joy may be full.*

Daniel 9:18... *We do not ask these things because we are good; instead, we ask because of your mercy. (New Century Version)*

James 5:16... *When a believing person prays, great things happen. (New Century Version)*

James 4:3... *Or when you ask, you do not receive because the reason you ask is wrong. You want things so you can use them for your own pleasures. (New Century Version)*

Colossians 4:2... *Don't be weary in prayer; keep at it; watch for God's answers, and remember to be thankful when they come. (The Living Bible)*

Matthew 26:41... *Keep alert and pray. Otherwise temptation will overpower you. For the spirit indeed is willing, but how weak the body is! (The Living Bible)*

1 Timothy 2:8... *So I want men everywhere to pray with holy hands lifted up to God, free from sin and anger and resentment. (The Living Bible)*

Matthew 6:9-13... *After this manner therefore pray ye: Our Father which art in heaven, Hallowed be thy name. Thy kingdom come. Thy will be done in earth, as it is in heaven. Give us this day our daily bread. And forgive us our debts, as we forgive our debtors. And lead us not into temptation, but deliver us from evil: For thine is the kingdom, and the power, and the glory, for ever. Amen.*

Personal Notes & Thoughts

God's Gift: The Holy Spirit

The Holy Spirit is the third person of the Godhead. In simple terms, He co-exists with the Father and the Son. In other words, He is one with God, the Father and Jesus Christ, His Son. He is also called the Holy Ghost and the Comforter. Jesus promised to send Him to the disciples after His crucifixion and resurrection.

It is important to note that the Holy Spirit is a "He" not an "it!" He has a will and He is intellectual which means you can offend the Holy Spirit. He is involved intimately in your life which means He knows and understands everything about you and is committed to helping you walk in obedience to God's Word. He will bring you to a place of conviction, making you aware of when you do wrong but also showing you how to get back on track.

He also teaches and encourages you so that you will be fully equipped to do God's Kingdom work. He enables you to do this by giving you special abilities — spiritual gifts. These spiritual gifts empower you to complete your God-given assignment in the earth. Possessing these spiritual gifts through the Holy Spirit will also help you to build up the Body of Christ — His church. The Bible mentions many gifts and the Holy Spirit will make clear to you what your gift/s are.

In essence, the Holy Spirit is an essential ingredient for the Christian life enabling you to be effectual in your service to God. The Holy Spirit supplies you with that much needed power of God, giving you the confidence and courage to stand in the name of Jesus Christ and do His divine will.

The Holy Spirit is a wonderful gift from God given to us so that we can receive continual direction for holy living. Now that you have professed belief in Jesus Christ and made a commitment to be His disciple and follow Him, the Holy Spirit is yours to receive. Just pray and ask God to fill you with His Holy Spirit and He will.

Read what the Bible says...

Acts 1:8... *But ye shall receive power, after that the Holy Ghost is come upon you: and ye shall be witnesses unto me both in Jerusalem, and in all Judaea, and in Samaria, and unto the uttermost part of the earth.*

Romans 8:26... *And in the same way — by our faith — the Holy Spirit helps us with our daily problems and in our praying. For we don't even know what we should pray for nor how to pray as we should, but the Holy Spirit prays for us with such feeling that it cannot be expressed in words. (The Living Bible)*

Acts 2:1-4... *When the day of Pentecost came, they were all together in one place. Suddenly a noise like a strong, blowing wind came from heaven and filled the whole house where they were sitting. They saw something like flames of fire that were separated and stood over each person there. They were all filled with the Holy Spirit, and they began to speak different languages by the power the Holy Spirit was giving them. (New Century Version)*

Acts 2:38, 39... *Then Peter said unto them, Repent, and be baptized every one of you in the name of Jesus Christ for the remission of sins, and ye shall receive the gift of the Holy Ghost. For the promise is unto you, and to your children, and to all that are afar off, even as many as the Lord our God shall call.*

Romans 8:11... *And if the Spirit of God, who raised up Jesus from the dead, lives in you, he will make your dying bodies live again after you die, by means of this same Holy Spirit living within you. (The Living Bible)*

1 Corinthians 12:8-11... *To one person the Spirit gives the ability to give wise advice; someone else may be especially good at studying and teaching, and this is his gift from the* *same Spirit. He gives special faith to another, and to someone else the power to heal the sick. He gives power for doing miracles to some, and to others power to prophesy and preach. He gives someone else the power to know whether evil spirits are speaking through those who claim to be giving God's messages-or whether it is really the Spirit of God who is speaking. Still another person is able to speak in languages he never learned; and others, who do not know the language either, are given power to understand what he is saying. It is the same and only Holy Spirit who gives all these gifts and powers, deciding which each one of us should have. (The Living Bible)*

Ephesians 4:11-13... *Some of us have been given special ability as apostles; to others he has given the gift of being able to preach well; some have special ability in winning people to Christ, helping them to trust him as their Savior; still others have a gift for caring for God's people as a shepherd does his sheep, leading and teaching them in the ways of God. Why is it that he gives us these special abilities to do certain things best? It is that God's people will be equipped to do better work for him, building up the Church, the body of Christ, to a position of strength and maturity; until finally we all believe alike about our salvation and about our Savior, God's Son, and all become full-grown in the Lord-yes, to the point of being filled full with Christ. (The Living Bible)*

Also read the following: Romans 12:3-8

Personal Notes & Thoughts

Fellowship

Fellowship — Being in the company of other Christians helps you to grow and mature in your new faith. It is important to interact with other believers coming together in an environment of like-minded people. Now that you are a Christian you will find that your moral standards and beliefs will often be very different to those around you. In order to stay firm in your new found faith, you will need the help of your new Christian family and friends. You can get together and discuss, learn from and compare notes with each other. Sharing testimonies and personal experiences can also be a great source of encouragement. It's fun and interesting to find out how everyone is enjoying their relationship and life with their new friend, Jesus.

Read what the Bible says...

Psalm 122:1... *I was glad when they said unto me, Let us go into the house of the Lord.*

Psalm 133:1... *Behold, how good and how pleasant it is for brethren to dwell together in unity!*

Hebrews 10:25... *Not forsaking the assembling of ourselves together, as the manner of some is; but exhorting one another: and so much the more, as ye see the day approaching.*

Ephesians 5:15—20... *So be careful how you act; these are difficult days. Don't be fools; be wise: make the most of every opportunity you have for doing good. Don't act thoughtlessly, but try to find out and do whatever the Lord wants you to. Don't drink too much wine, for many evils lie along that path; be filled instead with the Holy Spirit and controlled by him. Talk with each other much about the Lord, quoting psalms and hymns and singing sacred songs, making music in your hearts to the Lord. Always give thanks for everything to our God and Father in the name of our Lord Jesus Christ. (The Living Bible)*

Romans 12:4... *Just as there are many parts to our bodies, so it is with Christ's body. We are all parts of it, and it takes every one of us to make it complete, for we each have different work to do. So we belong to each other, and each needs all the others. (The Living Bible)*

1 Thessalonians 5:11... *So encourage each other to build each other up, just as you are already doing. (The Living bible)*

Acts 2:42... *They joined with the other believers in regular attendance at the apostles' teaching sessions and at the Communion services and prayer meetings. (The Living Bible)*

1 Corinthians 14:26... *Well, my brothers, let's add up what I am saying. When you meet together some will sing, another will teach, or tell some special information God has given him, or speak in an unknown language, or tell what someone else is saying who is speaking in the unknown language, but everything that is done must be useful to all, and build them up in the Lord. (The Living Bible)*

Proverbs 27:17... *As iron sharpens iron, so people can improve each other. (New Century Version)*

Personal Notes & Thoughts

Make A Joyful Noise!

Praising and worshipping the Lord is our way of telling God how great He is and how much we love Him. True worship comes from your heart. It is not forced — It is spontaneous coming from a place of genuine appreciation for who God is in your life. Praise and Worship should become as natural to you as brushing your teeth! It should be something you get into the habit of doing every single day.

Offering up Praise and Worship to God is one of the greatest secrets of constant spiritual victory. Having the 'Attitude of Gratitude' to God will be a fantastic witness to others of how much you appreciate the goodness and grace that He gives you daily. How awesome it would be if others are also encouraged to connect and commend the

God that you praise, worship and serve — Being inspired to take the same step to salvation that you have.

Read what the Bible says...

Psalm 50:23... *But true praise is a worthy sacrifice; this really honors me. Those who walk my paths will receive salvation from the Lord. (The Living Bible)*

Psalm 92:1, 2 ... *It is a good thing to give thanks unto the Lord, and to sing praises unto thy name, O most High: To shew forth thy loving kindness in the morning, and thy faithfulness every night*

Psalm 103:1-5... *I bless the holy name of God with all my heart. Yes, I will bless the Lord and not forget the glorious things he does for me. He forgives all my sins. He heals me. He ransoms me from hell. He surrounds me with loving-kindness and tender mercies. He fills my life with good things! My youth is renewed like the eagle's! (The Living Bible)*

Hebrews 13:15... *With Jesus' help we will continually offer our sacrifice of praise to God by telling others of the glory of his name. (The Living Bible)*

1 Thessalonians 5:18... *In every thing give thanks: for this is the will of God in Christ Jesus concerning you.*

Philippians 4:4... *Rejoice in the Lord alway: and again I say, Rejoice.*

Personal Notes & Thoughts

Your Personal Sacrifice...

In the Old Testament God's people sacrificed animals to God to atone for their sins. In God's redemption plan for mankind Jesus Christ made himself a sacrifice for the sins of the whole world so we no longer have to sacrifice animals. Now we offer ourselves, our lives to God as a living sacrifice. We don't have to actually end our lives to make this sacrifice but in faith we offer every part of ourselves for God's holy use.

The Word of God encourages us to live holy lives. In essence we are offering our bodies completely unto the Lord. Every day you should ask the Lord to make and mould you into a pure vessel available for Him to use for His work here on Earth.

When you pray, tell the Lord that His divine will is your will — that you have chosen to give Him control over your thoughts, the words you speak and over the things you do. You are simply saying that Jesus directs your every moment and your future is in His hands. If you learn to live a pure and holy life then God can live in you guiding you each day.

Read what the Bible says...

Romans 12:1, 2... *I beseech you therefore, brethren, by the mercies of God, that ye present your bodies a living sacrifice, holy, acceptable unto God, which is your reasonable service. And be not conformed to this world: but be ye transformed by the renewing of your mind, that ye may prove what is that good, and acceptable, and perfect, will of God.*

Luke 9:23... *Then he said to all, "Anyone who wants to follow me must put aside his own desires and conveniences and carry his cross with him every day and keep close to me! (The Living Bible)*

Proverbs 3:6... *In everything you do, put God first, and he will direct you and crown your efforts with success. (The Living Bible)*

Psalm 37:23, 24... *The steps of good men are directed by the Lord. He delights in each step they take. If they fall it isn't fatal, for the Lord holds them with his hand. (The Living Bible)*

2 Corinthians 6:16... *And what union can there be between God's temple and idols? For you are God's temple, the home of the living God, and God has said of you, "I will live in them and walk among them, and I will be their God and they shall be my people." (The Living Bible)*

Colossians 3:5-10... *So put all evil things out of your life: sexual sinning, doing evil, letting evil thoughts control you, wanting things that are evil, and greed. This is really serving a false god. These things make God angry. In your past, evil life you also did these things. But now also put these things out of your life: anger, bad temper, doing or saying things to hurt others, and using evil words when you talk. Do not lie to each other. You have left your old sinful life and the things you did before. You have begun to live the new life, in which you are being made new and are becoming like the One who made you. This new life brings you the true knowledge of God. (New Century Version)*

Personal Notes & Thoughts

Money Helps God's Word Go Round!

As a Christian, you should view the Kingdom responsibility of spreading the Gospel and all that it involves as the greatest work on earth but it is in great need of our financial support. Expenses are incurred in any type of business or organisation. To help to promote the Gospel of Jesus Christ we need to ensure that there is enough financial provision for the vision and this is where you can help.

As you grow and mature as a Christian, it is important to ensure that your Spirit of Giving grows too. Remember, the Lord loves and delights in a cheerful giver. We should be excited about contributing financially to God's Kingdom work in the earth. And don't forget... Your willingness to give to God will be rewarded. God promises to generously reward all those who give. We should also remember that giving is a form of worship and our heavenly Father loves when we worship Him.

There are special blessings prepared for those who give their tithe and offerings. Your tithe is 10% of any income you receive and your offering can be any amount that you decide or feel inspired to give. As we give, whatever amount it may be, the Lord warns us in his Word to ensure that we do not become puffed up with pride in our hearts.

As we give, we identify with the heart of God towards His work in the earth. We become burdened as we see the needs of the church. If you haven't started giving to the Lord through your new church home then you should begin! Prayerfully think about a commitment that you can make regularly. Then start giving it—God will bless you in amazing ways as you commit to giving to His Kingdom work.

Read what the Bible says...

Malachi 3:10, 11... *Bring to the storehouse a full tenth of what you earn so there will be food in my house. Test me in this," says the Lord All-Powerful. "I will open the windows of heaven for you and pour out all the blessings you need. I will stop the insects so they won't eat your crops. The grapes won't fall from your vines before they are ready to pick," says the Lord All-Powerful. (New Century Version)*

2 Corinthians 9:6, 7... *But this I say, He which soweth sparingly shall reap also sparingly; and he which soweth bountifully shall reap also bountifully. Every man according as he purposeth in his heart, so let him give; not grudgingly, or of necessity: for God loveth a cheerful giver.*

Acts 20:35... *I have shewed you all things, how that so labouring ye ought to support the weak, and to remember the words of the Lord Jesus, how he said, It is more blessed to give than to receive. (Also read Luke 6:33-35)*

Proverbs 3:9, 10... *Honour the Lord by giving him the first part of all your income, and he will fill your barns with wheat and barley and overflow your wine vats with the finest wines. (The Living Bible)*

2 Corinthians 8:7... *You are rich in everything — in faith, in speaking, in knowledge, in truly wanting to help, and in the love you learned from us. In the same way, be strong also in the grace of giving (New Century Version).*

Luke 6:38... *Give, and you will receive. You will be given much. Pressed down, shaken together, and running over, it will spill into your lap. The way you give to others is the way God will give to you. (New Century Version)*

1 Timothy 6:17... *Tell those who are rich not to be proud and not to trust in their money, which will soon be gone, but their pride and trust should be in the living God who always richly gives us all we need for our enjoyment. (The Living Bible)*

Personal Notes & Thoughts

Keep The Faith

I have mentioned faith in a few places throughout this book. I think this is a good place to deal with faith in more detail. As a new Christian it is hoped that you will grow in faith. In simple terms, your faith is your belief in God's promises, trusting in His faithfulness, and relying on Him to act on your behalf.

In Habakkuk 2:4 it says that the one who lives the right way and who is righteous will have a successful life because of his faith in God.

Your faith is your belief system. The more that you read God's Word, the more your faith will grow. Your trust and reliance in Jesus will increase. The Bible says that your faith comes by hearing and understanding the Word of

God so it is imperative that you read your Bible regularly.

It is important to realise that faith is one of the basic ingredients needed for a true relationship with God. You wouldn't want a relationship with someone you do not trust. You wouldn't want to be friends with someone you feel keeps lying to you. Your faith in God is the assurance that you believe the Bible is true. Your faith is the strong conviction you have that what God has promised will happen. It is having confidence in God even though there may not be any tangible proof. Faith is complete and unquestionable trust, confidence and reliance in your heavenly Father. You can also say that faith is the opposite of doubt.

Webster's Dictionary defines faith as "belief and trust in and loyalty to God; firm belief in something for which there is no proof; unquestioning belief that does not require proof or evidence."[1]

Your faith becomes more consistent as you continue in your Christian life and the more you act on your faith, the more confident you will become and the more your faith will grow. Very few have great faith straight away and that's fine as long as you do not give up because with time, the Holy Spirit will help your faith to grow and soon you will find yourself 'moving mountains!'

1 https://www.merriam-webster.com/dictionary

Read what the Bible says...

2 Corinthians 5:7... *For we walk by faith, not by sight.*

Matthew 21:22... *And all things, whatsoever ye shall ask in prayer, believing, ye shall receive.*

Hebrews 11:1, 6... *What is faith? It is the confident assurance that something we want is going to happen. It is the certainty that what we hope for is waiting for us, even though we cannot see it up ahead. You can never please God without faith, without depending on him. Anyone who wants to come to God must believe that there is a God and that he rewards those who sincerely look for him. (The Living Bible)*

Habakkuk 2:4... *The evil nation is very proud of itself; it is not living as it should. But those who are right with God will live by trusting in him. (New Century Version)*

Romans 10:17... *So faith comes from hearing, and hearing through the word of Christ. (English Standard Version)*

Mark 11:24... *Therefore I say unto you, What things soever ye desire, when ye pray, believe that ye receive them, and ye shall have them.*

Mark 9:24... *Immediately the father cried out, "I do believe! Help me to believe more!" (New Century Version)*

Personal Notes & Thoughts

Don't Relax—There Are Millions More...

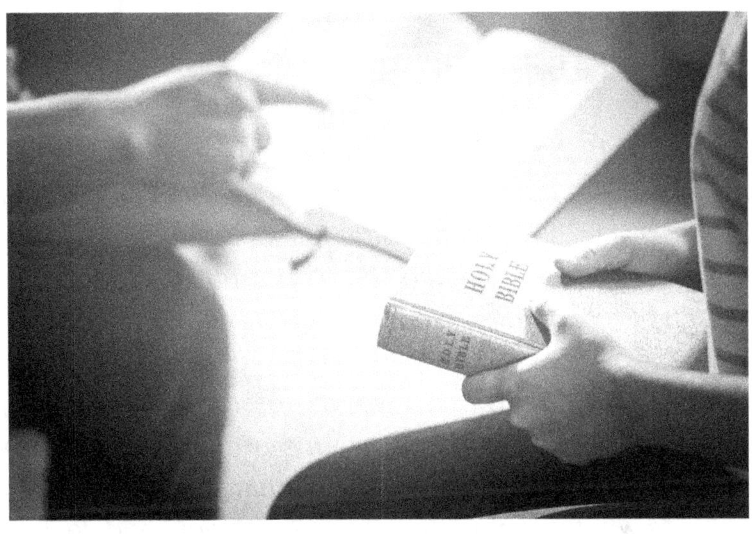

The winning or saving of lost souls is the dearest thing to the heart of the Father. He doesn't want any souls to be lost. This is not surprising when you remember that when Jesus died on the cross, the saving of souls was His sole purpose and focus. He died to pay the debt of sin for mankind so that we can be free from the penalty of death. Therefore, the main aim of your life should be the seeking of souls for God's Kingdom. You are now a follower of Jesus — one of His disciples which means you should be witnessing and telling others about Jesus so they can get to know Him too.

Men, women and young people who die without Christ —
Die without hope. Let your life, daily actions, testimonies
and accolades about God, be a witness to others. You can
show them the Peace, Love and Security that life with
Jesus Christ brings. In other words... Let your light shine!

Read what the Bible says...

John 3:16, 17... *For God loved the world so much that he
gave his only Son so that anyone who believes in him shall
not perish but have eternal life. For God sent not his Son
into the world to condemn the world; but that the world
through him might be saved. (The Living Bible)*

Matthew 28:19, 20... *Go ye therefore, and teach all
nations, baptizing them in the name of the Father, and of
the Son, and of the Holy Ghost: Teaching them to observe
all things whatsoever I have commanded you: and, lo, I am
with you alway, even unto the end of the world. Amen.*

Proverbs 11:30... *The fruit of the righteous is a tree of life;
and he that winneth souls is wise.*

Luke 10:1, 2... *The Lord now chose seventy other disciples
and sent them on ahead in pairs to all the towns and
villages he planned to visit later. These were his
instructions to them: "Plead with the Lord of the harvest to
send out more labourers to help you, for the harvest is so
plentiful and the workers so few. (The Living Bible)*

Mark 1:17... *Jesus called out to them, "Come, follow me! And I will make you fishermen for the souls of men!" (The Living Bible)*

Matthew 5:14-16... *"You are the light that gives light to the world. A city that is built on a hill cannot be hidden. And people don't hide a light under a bowl. They put it on a lampstand so the light shines for all the people in the house. In the same way, you should be a light for other people. Live so that they will see the good things you do and will praise your Father in heaven. (New Century Version)*

1 Peter 3:15... *But respect Christ as the holy Lord in your hearts. Always be ready to answer everyone who asks you to explain about the hope you have. (New Century Version)*

Romans 10:15... *And how will anyone go and tell them unless someone sends him? That is what the Scriptures are talking about when they say, "How beautiful are the feet of those who preach the Gospel of peace with God and bring glad tidings of good things." In other words, how welcome are those who come preaching God's Good News! (The Living Bible)*

Acts 1:8... *But ye shall receive power, after that the Holy Ghost is come upon you: and ye shall be witnesses unto me both in Jerusalem, and in all Judaea, and in Samaria, and unto the uttermost part of the earth.*

Personal Notes & Thoughts

Conclusion

You have a new life! You are now a new creation in Jesus Christ (2 Corinthians 5:17). He promises to be a real friend to you and to be with you always. Your Bible is your guide to finding out all about Him and how to live as a Christian. It is important that you spend time reading your Bible, praying and doing all the things that you have read about in this book. Your future as an effective Christian is dependent on your consistent faith walk with God.

As you embark on your new life with Christ don't expect to get things right straight away! Sometimes you may make mistakes and feel absolutely awful but remember not to base your Christian life on just feelings. Sometimes you will feel God's presence and be reassured but there may be other times when you do not feel that God is close and may question whether you are really saved. It's not about your feelings — it's about your faith. It's about trusting God's Word and believing that what the Bible says is true.

Sometimes it can take a while before the old habits of many years are replaced with the new behaviour of a Christ-like life. Jesus will teach you, speaking to you through His Word and His Holy Spirit, whom He has sent to be with you always. He will show you all that you need to know and be that much needed support in difficult times. Always remember this—

> ## A Successful Christian Life Is Lived...
> ## One day At A Time!

I have one more Bible verse for you to note. It will help you stay focused positively each day... Philippians 4 v 8

Finally, brethren, whatsoever things are true,
whatsoever things are honest,
whatsoever things are just,
whatsoever things are pure,
whatsoever things are lovely,
whatsoever things are of good report;
if there be any virtue,
and if there be any praise,
think on these things.

Thoughts & Declarations
For Each Day

- With the help of God's Word I know that I am now saved

- I will not give in to feelings of doubt, disappointment or discouragement or any other feelings or emotions that hinder my Christian walk

- God is my heavenly Father and He loves and cares for me

- I am entitled to receive God's blessings

- I will give all my worries and cares to my friend and constant companion, Jesus Christ

- I know that I have God's total protection and I will no longer fear the devil

- I am willing to follow Christ' example through water baptism

- I will receive Holy Communion regularly

- I will read God's Word, the Bible daily

- I will pray regularly and work on deepening my relationship with God

- I will fellowship with other Christians

- I will always praise and worship God

- I offer and present my entire being daily to the Lord Jesus Christ for His Kingdom purpose

- I will embrace a Spirit of Giving and give regularly to the work of God

- I have faith. I will live by what I believe and not by what I can see

- I will tell others about Jesus and how He can change their lives for the better

References Sources

The Holy Bible

World Wide Web (www)

PC Study Bible Version 5 (www.biblesoft.com)